LEON DRAISAITL

HOCKEY SUPERSTAR

BY ROY RATHBURN

Book design by Jake Nordby
Cover design by Jake Nordby

Photographs ©: Jason Franson/The Canadian Press/AP Images, cover, 1, 6; Codie McLachlan/Getty Images Sport/Getty Images, 4–5, 23, 26–27; Mitchell Leff/Getty Images Sport/Getty Images, 8; Lukasz Laskowski/PressFocus/MB Media/Getty Images Sport/Getty Images, 11; Bruce Bennett/Getty Images Sport/Getty Images, 13; Derek Leung/Getty Images Sport/Getty Images, 14; Marissa Baecker/Getty Images Sport/Getty Images, 17; Rocky W. Widner/NHL/Getty Images Sport/Getty Images, 18; Paul Sancya/AP Images, 20–21, 30; Ethan Miller/Getty Images Sport/Getty Images, 25; Red Line Editorial, 29

Press Box Books, an imprint of Press Room Editions, Inc.

ISBN
978-1-63494-871-5 (library bound)
978-1-63494-889-0 (paperback)
978-1-63494-923-1 (epub)
978-1-63494-907-1 (hosted ebook)

Library of Congress Control Number: 2023922032

Distributed by North Star Editions, Inc.
2297 Waters Drive
Mendota Heights, MN 55120
www.northstareditions.com

Printed in the United States of America
082024

About the Author

Roy Rathburn is a retired English teacher and former hockey player, coach, and official, from northern Minnesota.

TABLE OF CONTENTS

29
29
29
OILERS
WARRIOR
WARRIOR

1 THE JUMP START

A fortunate bounce placed the puck at the skates of Leon Draisaitl. His speed and skill took over from there. The Edmonton Oilers star raced between two Anaheim Ducks and toward the net.

Edmonton's 2017 playoff run was on the brink. With another loss to the Ducks, the season would be over. Less than three minutes into the game, Draisaitl gave Oilers fans hope.

Draisaitl left the defenders in the dust. Now it was just him and the goaltender.

Leon Draisaitl recorded 16 points in 13 games during the 2017 playoffs.

Draisaitl celebrates after scoring one of his three goals against the Ducks.

Draisaitl shot the puck between the goalie's legs and into the net. Edmonton now had a 1–0 lead.

Minutes later, Draisaitl gathered a loose puck in front of the goal. A defender quickly cut off his angle to shoot. But Draisaitl didn't let that stop him. He spun to his backhand and guided the puck into the goal. The young center had just put Edmonton ahead 2–0.

The Oilers raced out to a 6–1 lead. But Draisaitl was still looking for his hat trick. Late in the second period, Draisaitl fed the puck to teammate Milan Lucic. Then Lucic passed the puck right back to Draisaitl, who was all alone in the slot.

Draisaitl one-timed the puck to beat the goalie. It was his first playoff hat trick. More importantly, the Oilers lived to play another day. And it was their new star who gave them the boost they needed.

GREAT LIKE GRETZKY

Draisaitl became the first Oiler to score a hat trick in the playoffs in 17 years. And he did it at the age of 21. Only one Oiler had been younger when scoring a playoff hat trick. It was "The Great One" himself, Wayne Gretzky.

2 CROSSING THE POND

Leon Draisaitl was born in Cologne, Germany, on October 27, 1995. Leon's dad, Peter, was playing pro hockey there. Peter taught his son to skate at a young age. When Leon first played hockey, he would start to cry when he had all his gear on. He just wanted to go home. But before long, Leon was begging his dad not to leave the rink. Once Leon got a bit older, he enjoyed spending time around his dad's team and learning from the pros.

Leon Draisaitl first played with the German senior national hockey team in 2014.

In Germany, soccer is the most popular sport. Leon played soccer for a while. He tried other sports, too. But he loved hockey the most. Having his dad as a teacher helped a lot.

From an early age, Leon scored goals with ease. He also helped set up teammates for scoring chances. In the 2010–11 season, Leon recorded 97 goals and 95 assists. And he did it in just 29 games.

Though he was still a teenager, Leon was ready for a new challenge. At the age of 16, he moved across the Atlantic Ocean to play in Canada. Canada's junior hockey leagues were

GERMAN HOCKEY LEGENDS

Peter Draisaitl was born in Czechoslovakia. He never played in the NHL. But he was well known to German hockey fans. He represented Germany at three Winter Olympics. He also had a long pro career in the German league. The Draisaitl name became even more famous in Germany when Peter's son, Leon, went pro.

Leon Draisaitl played in six different international tournaments before he entered the NHL.

some of the best in the world. Leon joined the Prince Albert Raiders of the Western Hockey League (WHL). He was taking the next step toward someday playing in the National Hockey League (NHL).

It was tough for Leon to move away from home at such a young age. He had to grow up quickly, both in life and in hockey. Even so, Leon had a solid first season with the Raiders. In 64 games, he tallied 21 goals and 37 assists. The next year, he broke out with 38 goals and 67 assists.

NHL teams had taken notice of Leon's skills. The young center had grown to 6-foot-2 (188 cm) and weighed more than 200 pounds (91 kg). On top of his size, Leon possessed great skating and playmaking abilities. Shortly after Leon's second season with the Raiders, the Edmonton Oilers selected him with the third overall pick in the 2014 NHL Entry Draft.

Leon Draisaitl (right) became the highest-drafted player out of Germany in NHL history when the Oilers selected him in 2014.

OILERS

OILERS
29
CCM
CANADA

3 NEW HEIGHTS

Leon Draisaitl had proved he belonged at each level of hockey he'd tried. But the next level was the toughest yet. Draisaitl had to show he belonged in the NHL as an 18-year-old rookie.

Draisaitl made his NHL debut in the first game of the 2014–15 season. However, it took time to adjust to the NHL. He didn't score his first goal until the eighth game. And after 37 games, he had scored just one more goal. Due to his slow start, Edmonton sent him back down to

Draisaitl tallied only nine points as a rookie in 2014–15.

junior hockey. The Oilers thought he needed more time to develop.

Playing for the Kelowna Rockets, Draisaitl dominated again at the junior level. He led the Rockets to the league championship. And he was named Most Valuable Player (MVP) of the playoffs.

When the 2015–16 season began, Draisaitl returned to the NHL. It took him just one game to match his goal total from the previous year. Draisaitl went on to have a solid season, finishing with 51 points in 72 games. It was also the start of his partnership with high-scoring Oilers center Connor McDavid. Together, they became one of the top-scoring duos in the NHL.

In the 2015 WHL playoffs, Draisaitl recorded 28 points in 19 games.

CCM
29

Connor McDavid (left) and Draisaitl combined to score 177 points during the 2016–17 season.

In 2016–17, Draisaitl and McDavid led the Oilers to their first playoff appearance in 11 years. Draisaitl's hat trick in Game 6 of the second round kept the Oilers alive against the Anaheim Ducks. However, the Ducks eliminated Edmonton in Game 7.

After the season, Draisaitl signed an eight-year contract worth $68 million. That was a lot of money for a player so early in his career. But the Oilers believed Draisaitl would only get better.

In the first year of his new deal, Draisaitl struggled. His scoring dropped as he played through injuries. The Oilers also struggled as a team. After taking a big step forward in 2016–17, the next season was a step back. Fans worried that Draisaitl's big contract might have been a mistake.

ASSISTING THE COMMUNITY

Draisaitl wanted to share some of his money with his community. In 2018, Draisaitl announced he would donate $1.2 million to Edmonton charities over the eight years of his contract. The money went toward encouraging kids in Canadian schools to get involved with volunteer work from a young age.

29

4 THE MVP

Leon Draisaitl wasn't feeling any extra pressure from his contract. He wanted to do his best no matter what. And he went into 2018–19 with confidence. The result was a historically good season. In the last game of the year, Draisaitl became just the sixth Oiler in history to score 50 goals in a season. That doubled the amount of goals he'd scored the season before.

Draisaitl's leadership began to stand out as well. While McDavid served as

The 2018–19 season was the first in Draisaitl's career where he tallied more than 100 points.

captain, Draisaitl became an assistant captain before the 2019–20 season. The two players were a huge part of Edmonton's championship hopes. McDavid was usually the top scorer on the team. But that changed in 2019–20 when Draisaitl broke out with his best season yet. His 110 points led the entire NHL. Draisaitl's impressive numbers earned him the Hart Trophy as MVP of the league. He became the first German to win the award.

Draisaitl took pride in the individual awards. But what he wanted most was a Stanley Cup. In 2020–21, Edmonton finished seventh in the NHL in scoring.

MR. GERMANY

As one of the greatest German hockey players ever, Draisaitl has emerged as a leader on the German national team. He has played in several World Championships as well as youth tournaments. Draisaitl has also helped bring the NHL to Germany. In 2018, the Oilers traveled to Draisaitl's hometown to play an exhibition game.

Draisaitl recorded 25 assists in the 2022 playoffs. That led the entire NHL.

However, the team didn't win a single game in the playoffs.

The 2021–22 season was a different story. Draisaitl set a new career high with 55 goals in the regular season. Then the Oilers met the

Los Angeles Kings in the first round of the playoffs. Edmonton won the series, but Draisaitl hurt his ankle. In the next round, he battled through the pain as the Oilers faced their biggest rival, the Calgary Flames.

Draisaitl wasn't slowed down at all. He scored just two goals in the series. But his 15 assists were the most ever for a player in a playoff series. The Oilers beat the Flames in five games.

Edmonton was one series away from playing in the Stanley Cup Final. Draisaitl recorded six assists as he played through more pain. But the Oilers couldn't manage a win against the Colorado Avalanche.

The following season, Draisaitl again set a new career high with 128 points. However, the Oilers lost in the second round of the playoffs.

Draisaitl scored 13 goals in 12 games during the 2023 playoffs.

The loss hurt. But with Draisaitl and McDavid leading the way, Oilers fans believed a Stanley Cup victory was possible.

TAKE A SEAT

Leon Draisaitl camped in front of the net in a 2023 playoff game against the Los Angeles Kings. In an act of desperation, a Kings player tripped Draisaitl while he shot. But the puck went in. Draisaitl celebrated while sitting on the ice.

TIMELINE

1. **Cologne, Germany (October 27, 1995)**
   Leon Draisaitl is born.

2. **Prince Albert, Saskatchewan (September 20, 2013)**
   Leon plays in his first game with the Prince Albert Raiders.

3. **Philadelphia, Pennsylvania (June 27, 2014)**
   The Edmonton Oilers select Draisaitl third overall in the NHL Entry Draft.

4. **Edmonton, Alberta (October 9, 2014)**
   Draisaitl plays in his first NHL game.

5. **San Jose, California (April 22, 2017)**
   Draisaitl scores a goal to help the Oilers beat the San Jose Sharks and win a playoff series for the first time since 2006.

6. **Chicago, Illinois (March 5, 2020)**
   Draisaitl records two assists, giving him 110 points for the season to lead the NHL. Draisaitl is later awarded the Hart Trophy as the MVP of the league.

7. **Calgary, Alberta (May 26, 2022)**
   Draisaitl records his 15th assist in a playoff series against the Calgary Flames, setting an all-time record for assists in a single series.

MAP

AT A GLANCE

Birth date: October 27, 1995

Birthplace: Cologne, Germany

Position: Center

Shoots: Left

Size: 6-foot-2 (188 cm), 208 pounds (94 kg)

NHL team: Edmonton Oilers (2014–)

Previous teams: Prince Albert Raiders (2012–14), Kelowna Rockets (2014–15)

Major awards: Hart Memorial Trophy (2020), Ted Lindsay Award (2020), Art Ross Trophy (2020), NHL All-Star (2019–20, 2022–23)

Accurate through the 2022–23 season.

GLOSSARY

backhand
The outside of the stick blade.

captain
A player who serves as the leader of a team.

contract
A written agreement that keeps a player with a team for a certain amount of time.

debut
First appearance.

draft
An event that allows teams to choose new players coming into the league.

exhibition
A game where the result does not affect the standings.

hat trick
When a player scores three or more goals in a game.

one-timed
Shot the puck directly from a pass without controlling it first.

rookie
A first-year player.

slot
The area in front of the goalkeeper and between the two face-off circles.

TO LEARN MORE

Books

Coleman, Ted. *Edmonton Oilers*. Mendota Heights, MN: Press Box Books, 2023.

Hanlon, Luke. *Wayne Gretzky: Hockey Legend*. Mendota Heights, MN: Press Box Books, 2024.

Stabler, David. *Meet Connor McDavid: Edmonton Oilers Superstar*. Minneapolis: Lerner Publications, 2024.

More Information

To learn more about Leon Draisaitl, go to **pressboxbooks.com/AllAccess**.

These links are routinely monitored and updated to provide the most current information available.

INDEX